ART OF BLOOD

Art of Blood

PERCEPTION *of*
REALITY PART 1

TWO FIVE

Palmetto Publishing Group
Charleston, SC

The Art of Blood
Copyright © 2020 by Two Five
All rights reserved

First Edition

Printed in the United States

ISBN-13: 978-1-64990-045-6
ISBN-10: 1-64990-045-7

ACKNOWLEDGEMENTS

An idea created from the individual mind, is a Reflection of The Most High Mind Almighty. The Art of Blood Reflects The Voice And or The /InFluences, Experiences Of The Warriors Who Best Represent The Tribe...Peace Almighty To Quest M. (and Jackson St. Damus in Yonkers New York)Who Chose me 21 Gun Salute +Years !Salute To my Elder Soul B. And The Whole Wazimu MBWA Family Askari For Life! Damu penda To All The Warriors worldwide Who Have Given up Blood, Sweat, and Tears on the Street and In the Prison System For The Cause And Not the Applause...B.i.p. SI salute To The Ubn ReD FlAg Vanguard BoW To THE Five! SaLute To The Whole oF NYB...B.i.p.Lord Lava (BBA) B.i.p.BIGTWo Five. BSV (Mount Vernon NEw York) B.i.p.T.Byrd 252, B.i.p.TajMahall(GSHINE) Salute To My Komrades In Arizona, All Damu HooDS & Districts Right Hand Spiral Power To The MotherLand B'S (California)THe Cultural Bearers of Blood Tree Rooted in Which We Are All For One , One For All!

ReDBrickSociety548" Keep Building The Black Pyramid...Last But not Least, Salute To the Founders Of BlooD "OH Almighty Let it Be Written Across All Sands and Lands. Ye Are The Creators Of Civilization The Builders/Healers And Protectors oF The Planet Earth . Do well To Inspire A Positive Movement At All Times. KEEP Our Youth LiBERATED Both Mentally & PHYSICALLY And out of the Hands Of Our OppRessor. One Love From Your Komrade Two Five

Peace!

CONTENTS

Tree of Life   1

Pyramid Reflections   9

One Blood   19

Red Flag   37

Five Point Star   43

Tree of Life

POEM

Rekindle ignite excite and unite the flame of our Askar.Spirit.
My mind grasps the vessels of the Un-seen.
My heart pumps Bloody Red Fluid. Right to Left.
Blood in essence is all a calculated rhythm
Left to Right
My soul embodies the Principle of Eternity
Light of my pyramid (temple) Fire in the middle.
Hated by many
Loved by few
Reflected by all
Life of a Damu...

Forever One Blood
Peace Almighty
Two Five

TREE OF LIFE

We benefit from every tree around us. Yes, trees produce fruits and vegetables. Even economic currency is made from trees but the most important element of life is oxygen, we receive from trees that nurture the spirit, Our levels of understanding becomes unlimited when we sprout out towards the sun radiating rapidly vibrations at a perfect rhythm, penetrating our home planet Earth.

It has always been known since the circum-navigation of Alkebulan the deity of gender. Unification of energy in everything that exists: masculinity by way of femininity. On the physical plane of our understanding this is sex (reproduction) man and woman. Opposites attract. Identical in nature (human beings) yet differing in physical degree. Duality complimenting the power of one.

Queen Sheba kissed by the sun in her natural attire, her body illuminated with the rays of love, jewel beads of ruby red around her neck. Divine protection hidden in the heart of her crown. Queen Sheba in her natural state of royalty began research to to find and unite mentally, physically, and spiritually with a king worthy of her soul. Much had been said of King Solomon, so the Queen inquired. King Solomon is said to have passed all the kings of the earth in riches and divine wisdom.

Queen Sheba sent forth scribes to King Solomon for a royal invite to his palace. The King accepted. Queen Sheba brought with her gifts such as spices, gold, and precious stones. Instantly the King and Queen communed near the olive tree under the morning star. The King answered all of the Queens questions and quickly the Queen realized the Kings wisdom. King Solomon gave Queen Sheba all of her desire - whatsoever she asked. Queen Sheba revealed to King Solomon that all of the greatness she had heard of him was accurate. But their embrace served a better purpose. A woman embraces her royalty and captures the heart of a king. A man elevates his mind and builds his world around a queen.

The principle of this story is dedicated to love, peace, and unity amongst the Blood family. We are righteous people. We are people determined to stand strong through all times of strife. A son and daughter learn their lessons seen and heard by mother and father. Inside the palace is it vital that a father demonstrates and teaches the son how to rekindle the inner warrior, how to love, respect, and protect a woman. And how to create a state of harmony when there's conflict within the tribe. In the same respect a woman must show the daughter how to carefully choose a man and how compromise for the better of the family brings positive results. And that a woman's womb and mind are the doors to her temple.

DAMU PENDA

Damu Penda: translates to blood love in the language of Swahili in Africa.

Damu Penda is an action word. A family affair. It represents a divine love beyond our being. Therefore there are no limitations or restraints when expressing our "love". We must never allow existing conditions of atrocity to impair our appreciation for one another. Damu Penda has the power to transform into a transcendence level of personal and unified development. Damu I am U, U are me, We are one. (in reflection) Repeat after me: I embrace the King in you, I embrace the Queen in you. Together we embrace our royalty in each other. Our values/principles reflect high character. A definition of the whole. Demonstrations of a simple salute shows virtue in respect, virtue in trust, virtue in loyalty to the family. We must build each other in all areas of life. In our hearts we remain filled with Damu Penda for our elder warriors who opened the doors and paved the way multiplying endless possibilities for the new generation of young warriors. Damu Penda lives because of the brave and bold, we combine one mind, one body, one soul.

Alway and Forever
Damu Penda

Pyramid Reflections

3 DEGREES

All across the seven continents of the world, our ancestors have left behind ancient text engraved in stone for the people to use as a base. To reach higher planes of being, to become one with the creator. The unlimited possibilities of what can be done to improve culture(s) and ultimately hold as a whole united power we can and will generate to improve our livelihood. Inhale the living meditated phenomenon knowledge of self-mastery, of self, and self achievement.

"3" DEGREES OF SELF

1st Degree: Knowledge of self- to gain knowledge of self as a principle is to utilize the world built around you. To become in tuned with a sense of consciously being aware of your own existence. Is there a purpose I must seek out and fulfill? Why have or was I designed to uplift humanity? Knowledge of self constitutes infinite dimensions of mind power. Becoming receptive mentally, inducing mind of self to liberate invisible chains that hinder development. To have in your possession knowledge of self is to have knowledge of everything in existence because everything in existence is a reflection of self.

2nd Degree: Mastery of self- Knowledge. Wisdom. Understanding. You must grasp the scepter of power and command the body (vehicle) to channel the laws that govern everything. The supreme mind body in activation defined, distributes and directs elements of power that must be balanced within the body attributed to physical fitness. A master creates reality and remains in contact with the most high self, living proof of perfection.

3rd Degree: self achievement- represents the barriers/ struggles you overcame to present your contribution of art/craft. The steps of personal development, levels of divinity it takes to enter the doors of higher consciousness. Self achievement serves the purpose of concentrated effort, an investment towards destiny. History is recorded as we speak, as we listen, as we act. We have the power to define how we would want our legacy remembered. Written across the hearts and minds of all the people of the world.

A-Z ELEMENTS

A: Almighty- The source of creation: 'Man' the sole reflection of almighty on the physical plane. Knowledge of the universe is in the mastery of self.

B: BLOOD- Stream of knowledge directed by supreme intelligence. Substance, sustainable to the movement of the body.

C: Conscience- The resurrection of the 3rd eye (mind). With perception we are mobilized for positive action.

D: Damu- means BLOOD, warrior, Strength and Leadership in Swahili (African dialect). An original East African tribe in existence over 500 years.

E: Esoteric- strengthening spiritual and intellectual knowledge. Revealing truths once hidden.

F: Foundation- Applied knowledge orbits our temple. Each one- teach one- to reach one.

G: Guardians- It is our duty to protect and educate our family, communities, and nation. Guard the temple from outward forces of destruction.

H: Heart- The embodiment of divine power. Purification is achieved (assisted) by repetitive thoughts and genuine actions. Bearer of truth. Love and loyalty.

I: Immortality- Spiritual navigation. Mastering the laws of cause and effects.

J: Journey- The link of life's strand is connected in one phase. (Past- Present- and Future)

K: KMT- location of traditional spiritual education founded upon principles of nobility.

L: Love- The highest realization of life constitutes understanding an infinite balance based on truth.

M: Movement- Corresponding to the principles of vibration; rhythm. Tap into the frequencies of time and space enlightened mind of body.

N: Nation- people of the same family; cultural heritage, unity supported by identity.

O: Override- As warriors for the people we must do as much as possible to remove all barriers that guard oppression.

P: Power- The highest realization of self-application.

Q: Quest- Acquire profound elements in all wisdom there we will discover our seat of enlightenment.

R: Righteousness- Right state of mind, right conduct/ actions in all affairs.

S: Stars- Intertwined with the most high mind that operates rays of light representing divine consciousness. We are one with the entire universe.

T: Truth- about our meaning and purpose in life.

U: Understanding Unity Universe = Freedom

V: Victory- Mental streams of light expressed in spiritual and physical achievement.

W: Warrior- One who practices the forces of the intellect and skilled in the Art of War, for the benefit of restoring peace.

X: Xploration- Study the science of self (conscious) development (creation). Learn the truth about your existence and be free.

Y: Youth- Build the minds of our youth. Empower them today. It takes the whole village to raise our children.

Z: Zenith- The highest levels of achievement comes from practice, actions, and reflections. Build on, be strong.

5 PRINCIPLE OF LIBERATION
(Tano Nguzo Ya Uhuru)

1. Jitegemea- self reliance
2. Imani- faith
3. Umoja- unity
4. Ujima- collective work and responsibility
5. Ujamaa- cooperative economics

1. Self reliance- having confidence in the power of one's self. Activating the high frequencies through infinite dimensions confirmed within the mind. Become sole- controller of reality. Continuous efforts in forward direction.

2. Faith- Repetitive testimony based on previous results. Inner calling of power manifesting creativity in our physical reality.

3.   Unity- Union of our warriors spirit. U.N.I. stand together united through all levels of opposition we face. Unshakable foundation. The key to better livelihood.

4.   Collective work and responsibility- Lead by example. Exercising mind over matter. Utilizing our skills intelligently that best brings us forward to completing our goals. The pyramid built one brick at a time. The concept of communication.

5.   Cooperative Economics- Best represents our idea of building and creating our own businesses, that brothers and sisters can profit from together. Our gold (money) invested shines forth the road of promise secured for future generations. Allowing us to retire with the respect of our family, community and nation!

One Blood

B'S

Having been established since the first meeting represents the completion of the Red Alliance. We throw it up and lock the 'B' in unity in love and understanding of our purpose of existence symbolizing peace.

Our embrace symbolizes respect to the foundation and salute worthy 1,000 fold to our elders who understood why formation of a brotherhood was necessary. The 'B' is sacred and represents the link of time to our ancient order of civilization. We connect the 'B' of life to stay connected to our people in solidarity. For a cause as one body and to the highest degree of movement and strength.

Our precious blood is the cream filling of the universe. We hold the 'B's' high to the sky in principle of everything that ever was, is, a correspondent to the 'B'. The 'B's' penetrate rays of light through the puffy clouds uncovering any/all forms of deception. As above so below so below as above. At once it takes 8 minutes 20 seconds for the heart to pump blood within the body. The same amount of time it takes light from the sun to reach the earth. The circulation remains in motion. The 'B' being the living spirit of a nation. An everlasting concept of re-generation and connectedness of family.

B-Brotherly
L- Love
O-Override
O-Oppression
D-Destruction
S- Society

Brotherly- We are family BLOOD. Relatives and com-rades in arms for a common cause. We share a similar background and have experienced the same forms of pain. The same BLOOD that flows through your veins, runs through mines.

Love- A bond of shared emotional purity. Linking us as one. Love starts with the realization of self-value. Love is a form of inner peace. Outwardly expressed. Override- To ride over mentally and physically against all entities that serve the purpose of hindering the process of liberation. Resistance.

<u>Oppression</u>- Systematic adversity against the people in areas/institutions that promote education, law, economics, religion, and politics.

<u>Destruction</u>- Represents our vital awareness to recognize orchestrated plots by our oppressor to annihilate our people.

<u>Society</u>- Is us as a movement of the people for the people. A force designated by the people to bring forth positive results/actions against in-justices that do not serve our people.

SOULJAH STAGE 1ST LEVEL

SoulJah: This is the 1st step of being initiated after entering the door of the pyramid. A SoulJah learns what is necessary to study (practice) and trains under the guidance/wisdom of qualified generals. A SoulJah respects and obeys orders from generals. SoulJahs earns trust by displaying consistent demonstrations of loyalty. SoulJahs are persuaded into the right direction of the movement supplied with the tools to, to build for a purpose greater than themselves. A SoulJah protects the community. Honor, Respect, Trust, Loyalty, Love are unique qualities and principles embodied by a SoulJah. Armed with knowledge and faith a SoulJah can produce/or become of greater service to self, because everything a SoulJah experiences becomes a revelation. Every contribution of a SoulJah can directly add to the elevation of the family circle. Every SoulJah can and will contribute but to what degree, is measured by time as well as opportunity. May all actions be constructive.

A SoulJah trains to overcome obstacles and or weaknesses planted within the subconscious mind. This represents strength maximized at its potential and ability to incorporate supreme characteristics inherent of a true Askari (souljah/warrior).

GENERAL STAGE 2ND LEVEL

General: A general has mastered the characteristics of a SoulJah. A general is respected within the communities they reside. Generals have the duty of planning the daily activities with or alongside the SoulJahs to complete the mission at hand. Generals receive wisdom directly from the OG with careful observation. In light of being a commander, the general must be compassionate towards the SoulJahs and provide essential ingredients in respect towards mental and physical growth which is the natural way of life. Anything less is un-civilized. The general must be able to enforce the laws by example first but also be able to convey to the SoulJahs why the laws are important to follow/practice. Dealing with multiple personalities the general must exercise patience and develop methods that unify, specifically in times of emergency or exigent circumstances the SoulJahs that are most qualified should be in position to the place of the second level. The SoulJahs actions will reflect the mentorship received from the general. The general should strive for balance and secure victory against ignorance and poverty, those substances combined keep our people in the triple darkness: dumb, deaf, and blind. The general whether in peace or war does not allow anything negative to deter the positive movement. The general strides towards the vision with absolute purpose.

OG STAGE 3RD LEVEL

OG: serves as the prime example of success. Honored as such the SoulJah the general seeks the intellectual/spiritual guidance of the OG. An OG has what it takes to survive and also the experience to face all adversity/challenges. In order for the spirit (breath) of the movement to live and prosper the OG must share the necessary jewels by educating/directing those selected warriors destined to progress/elevate within the movement.

Our OG's are regarded with the highest respect. Without the OG's there would be no us. We call an OG an OG because of their sacrifices made to preserve tribal roots. Our OG's are the embodiment of the vessel containing enlightenment. Our OG's are there to support us, to provide and bestow upon us our history with the lessons so that we can devise/implement new plans or fresh tactics to accomplish greater achievements from generation to generation. So our OG's serve the purpose of strengthening our strategies when in search of answers and clarity. Our OG's are our link to the Past-Present-Future of our dynasty.

Love and respect to our OG's that are dead. Love and respect to our OG's living forever loyal to the cause. We will never forget your services and contributions.

DIALOGUE- DAMU AND BLOOD Q'S AND A'S 1-13

1. D. What is blood?

    B.Blood is the inception of our essence. Blood is compliments of supreme thoughts of the mind. Blood is consciousness flesh clothed within/without the body. Blood is knowledge. Blood is power. Blood is circulation. Blood is movement. Blood is universal. Blood is existence. And to conclude blood is everything in life.

2. D. Name some principles of blood?

    B.Unity. Love. Loyalty. Sacrifice.

3. D. What so these principles mean?

    B.Unity means togetherness/whole. As in united we must and shall stand strong. We are a movement of strength, divided by none. Love means pure in heart. The highest mental level of reality. In truth love is a bond that displays affection through creative expression. Loyalty means to stay firm. Solidarity. Even in the midst of adversity. Sacrifice means to invest mind, time, and energy as a tool towards accomplishment.

4. D. What does it mean to represent blood?

    B. To represent blood consists of a warrior mind frame. This isn't a part-time job, but to represent blood is a lifetime career. Blood is about realizing your purpose and working towards fulfilling it. To represent blood, you must be strong in mind, body, soul, heart and spirit.

5. D. How important is it for us to understand our history and lead by example?

    B. Our history supplies us the opportunity to evaluate our past consequences right and wrong. Also, to reflect plans of action here in the present. But with our determined will we can mold our place in the future. Our calling is linked to the communities: the hood-ghetto- slums- P.J(projects). The ones perceived to be the most disenfranchised, But there lies all the power. Individually and collectively we must seize our power and mobilize like never before. Our Black Panther Party stood up against the establishment of oppression and demonstrated positive struggle/efforts while mobilizing a vanguard for change. To include: educational programs- world politics- and history. Everything from socialism, economics to self-defense classes. Free breakfast programs- free clothing and health care clinics. These are examples of us defining ourselves and creating our own destiny. Remember Askari's(warriors). The elements of oppression still exist…

6. D. What is an oath?

B.An oath is a unique bond of testimony to ones' word embodied in truth. It is the decision to carry the burden of fulfilling a purpose or duty.

7. D. What is a pledge?

B.A pledge is a promise. A pledge is a devotion. A pledge is loyalty and the strength it takes to overcome adversity along the path of accomplishing goals and achievements.

8. 8.D. Define a prayer?

B.A prayer is a spiritual calling to the almighty spirit of the universe. United with daily practice, a prayer is actualized through meditation upon the inner will of heart, mind, and body.

9. D. Define the 3 elements?

B. 1) <u>Understanding:</u> embracing knowledge from use of personal experiences as well as wisdom gained from guidance of the elders.

2) <u>Structure:</u> Holding firm to establishment yet making adjustments when necessary to create the idea.

3) <u>Discipline:</u> Inner strength of one's capacity to maintain train of thought and action through times of challenge. This is mental and physical fitness.

10. D. What are some of the things Bloods can do to represent our tribe within the communities we came from?

B. It is important for us collectively to prioritize and contribute to the basic needs of the people which consist of food, clothing, and shelter. Social science. Communalism. Economic empowerment. Education with practice that ensures success. Bloods can continue to walk down all avenues of power that contribute to areas of development/change in society. A reflection of positive energy put forward. Bloods can be: Doctors, lawyers, Scientists, Teachers/professors, spiritual enlighteners, investors/bankers, community activists, environmental research specialists, politicians...However there are many other positions in society not named here but the point is clear. The way to make a difference is through constant application of right minded practices and procedures. Our warriors that guard the tribe from outward forces of oppression can teach the kids their existence is today's light, and carry with them the worlds legacy. We can continue to contribute to the maintenance of our community centers/institutions that reach out towards the betterment of our youth. Our youth need to know about teen pregnancy- Aids/H.I.V. awareness and its consequences. Self-defense classes that inspire physical fitness, Big Brother and Big Sister entrusted mentorship that deals with adulthood and family value. We are responsible for our kids guidance and protection in our tribe- communities- and nation! Soo Woop!

11. D. Many of our brothers and sisters are incarcerated, would you like to shed light or send some words of encouragement?

B.First, I salute all my ryders behind the wall who continue to stand tall and strong for what it 'B' like. Comrades keep battling those forces of oppression that exist in the belly of the beast. Second, stay focused on education. Education is a focus point due to the fact this allows us to be more productive, to evolve, to build inner strength, and refrain from thinking or feeling we have to stay engaged in crime or a criminal mindset. With education we know how to do better, We suffer from short term thinking and in the moment decisions that also inflicts pain upon the people we love. Overstand our ability to make a difference and stride our best foot forward starts within the inner dwelling of the mind. Warriors it is true we cannot always control the outcomes of situations we encounter. We can control how we respond by being prepared. Our brains function as a multi-dimensional level, which if carefully observed can correlate to a king or queen wearing a crown (upon the head). The crown symbolizes/ compliments the beauty and royalty or our minds. Our ability to sort out all problems dwelling within the mind. Life itself brothers and sisters in our physical form is an art (the mind at work) creation. Which gives power to the truth destiny is in our hands. Shape it as we will and improve our livelihood.

12. D. What other words of wisdom would you like to share regarding the importance of communication/ support of Bloods in prison and those still in the streets? B. Many times too often our Bloods behind the wall are neglected and abandoned. The same is true of our young bloods who don't fully comprehend the actuality of the causes we fight for in the streets. We are family and the only thing that can separate us is death. Even then we remain connected through the strand of our spirit. Inherently we know right from wrong. We have elders ready to share their wisdom (jewels), but we have to want it and be ready to listen. We must have the passion to perform daily with the right state of mind. It is treason to abandon our family/relatives in times of need. We must do individually all we can to take care of our brothers and sisters immediate needs regardless to where they may be, as well as send our love and support to their families. Our warriors have big hearts and in most cases share rolls of sole responsibility of keeping the family together as one. So when our dedicated brothers and sisters are in desperate need and distress situations we must always be of aide and assistance. None of our comrades are left stranded behind. No person, place, or thing can ever divide us. WE ALL WE GOT! Sometimes you sometimes me!

13. D. What role do Bloodettes have in the movement?

B. Our beloved sisters need to always be respected, protected, and honored as the royalty inherent of their essence. Our beginning. Our sisters have served and continue to serve the people in all areas of development. Our sisters are nurturers/ healers. They are our first teachers and everything we know concerning duties attributed to family household. With our sisters comes with the legacy of the movement. Life is strategy. As in the game of chess we want to reach higher levels/planes of existence. The king is in absolute control of the kingdom and what transpires on the battlefield. The queen his soulmate is the most powerful and secures the victory of the kingdom. This concept is a realization. Empower our Bloodette, we will experience the true glories in life.

7 CONCEPTS

1. Always in respect to the Damu nation. We always conduct ourselves in a righteous and just manner. We've always stood up against oppression and stood up for those who stand up for themselves. Which shows every element of our practice is a reflection recorded in the world we exist in.

2. In the name of Damu Beloved, no matter what set or hood we ryde for and come from it's always our individual duty to uphold our brothers and sisters in their absence. The same way we would do for self. By assuming the stance in unity is key to holding firm and overcoming any fragment of division. U-N-I-verse-all.

3. It is vital to always seek the counsel of our elders for guidance/direction. They possess sound wisdom gained directly from their experience. We must hold respect in our hearts for our elders who sacrificed their lives to make a difference for the upliftment of our movement.

4. To coincide with the stated above, loved ones we are

responsible for our levels of education and degree regarding steps to personal development. Study everything under the sun.

5. Love, Truth, Peace, Freedom, Justice are divine principles of culture. Practice them, lead by example. These keys open the door of liberation we seek in life.

6. Tread the paths of history and stay connected to the roots (source) of the tree. Build legal organizations of defense. Revolution has always been the strategy towards overcoming barriers for change.

7. We are tribal warriors with the duty of protecting our people against individualism and any other forces that subtract. Its not what the tribe does for you, its what you do for the tribe. Strive to hold firm to family obligations.

Red Flag

RED FLAG

The red flag beamed with light to bring forth acts of peace, or flamed with fire for war, life itself is governed by the law of balance. The RedFlag is rhythm. The RedFlag is movement. The RedFlag is circulation. Like that of the crystal skull. The RedFlag blazed with people inner-G, the RedFlag is vibration.

Guardians of the RedFlag possess the master keys to self liberation, ownership deals with responsibility that weighs deeply yet rotating within the dwelling of the subconscious mind. The RedFlag represents our innate abilities to act in accordance with what is naturally right to the right. The RedFlag is right on. The RedFlag speaks to the people. The power of the RedFlag reminds the brothers and the sisters that we have an honorable duty of restoring our people to their traditional heritage of greatness. The RedFlag is alive when you are alive spiritually, mentally, and physically. The RedFlag is rite of passage which can be seen as one with evolution, corresponding as an elevated or transitional phase from one life stage bound to another. In other words reflect into our train of thought. This is process of self-transformation, from pain, rage, and destruction to knowledge, wisdom, and understanding. The keys of life.

The RedFlag folded into its natural state of existence; the five and all its elements of power. Erected in stance 'A' alike to the building meaning, and reflection of the world pyramid. As well as the strength & effort of contribution to civilization! The Red represents the inner flow of blood throughout the body, within the blood and assessment of elements are billions of cells; the duality between peace and war. These cells consciously ward off diseases and toxins that would otherwise contribute to the demise of the body. The flag represents citizenship belonging to the spirit of the movement in the unity of the whole red nation! It represents the awakening. Resurrection of the original people/our tribal roots. The RedFlag represents danger/resistance to tyrants/oppressors that continue to seek the enslave the mind-body-soul.

The RedFlag represents the blood, sweat, tears shed in our past- present and future in our quest for liberation. Our RedFlag represents; Righteousness-state of mind demonstrated in actions that uplift the culture with the right sided practices. Order- Respect to our PYramid (fire in the middle) structure. In principle the body.

The RedFlag reflects the building of the whole which is one and the same our shared power the flag of red is equal to a road map of blood visible link/trace to ancestral roots.

Five Point Star

THE FIVE

Everything we relate to materially, spiritually, and even mentally can be added, reduced, multiplied and divided according to mathematics and science. We have developed ways to test- measure- and calculate everything pertaining to our physical existence to our benefit. But we also conclude due to constant study and practice as well as inner observation (divine touch) we are one with the movement/cosmic flow of the universe.

The five pointed star is mathematically correct and defines the cyclic evolution (up and down) of life. This is symbolic of humanity. This power is ever present and runs its course in spirals/circles. Patterns: birth-growth-aged-death-dust. THe lines between the points of the five pointed star connect 72 degree angles/space multiplied by the number '5' which equals 360 degrees evenly revealing completeness of a full circle. (72x5=360)

When observation of the universe has begun the stars reflect metaphysical distance yet its symbolism reveals an innate divinity tied to the mind's eye. The five represents love and unity. The five represents family. The five is balance that needs to be applied every sun light of our lives. The five represents the body: arm, leg, leg, arm, head. The five represents the activation/use of our five major senses which consists of sight, hearing, feeling, tasting, and smelling. The five is adaptability, the spinning wheel of our progress and growth.

The five symbolizes God in man of physical achievement followed by moral rectitude, inner and outer reflections of light (expression) where the union of physical and celestrial elements meet. Those five elements being: air, fire, water, earth, and ether are the building blocks of our world manifest. The five represents phases of life in one motion. Five is the apex of our pyramid.

FOOD FOR THOUGHT

Oppression is systematic adversity used as tools that represent our current status and existence. We become enslaved due to social-political and economic inequality. The worst form of oppression is a dysfunctional family indulging a sea of ignorance, a lack of unity amongst our own kind. We have inherited a generation of organized chaos which keeps the family in confusion. We must exercise/practice self-discipline. We must utilize lessons within our history as navigation of right conduct. We must stand unified in the name of Blood no matter if we are faced with 1,000 leagues of wrong practice. We will succeed, we will elevate by waves of right-hand spiral power, B's up! Restore the vision because: "Where there is no vision the people perish, but those that keepeth the law, happy are they" Proverbs 29:18

Our goal is and always has been devoted to 'Red' (Rising Every Damu) (freedom) Threefold: Spiritually, mentally and physically. Red is aligned with the duality of life's penetrating experiences of pain and power. Pain as in sacrifices that must be made in war. Power as in strength gained during and after we struggled to victory across the battlefield with our 'REDFLAG' high in honor of our nation across the globe...

www.ingramcontent.com/pod-product-compliance
Lightning Source LLC
Chambersburg PA
CBHW060237180626
46813CB00007B/3117

Art of Blood

One DAY at a time,
One STEP at a time,
One BRICK at a time.
Where do we start?
Just One at a TIME!

Palmetto
PUBLISHING GROUP
Made in Charleston, SC
www.PalmettoPublishingGroup.com

ISBN 978-1-64990-045-6

9 781649 900456